ERIC CARLE'S
BOOK OF MANY THINGS

WORLD OF ERIC CARLE
Penguin Young Readers Group
An Imprint of Penguin Random House LLC

To find out more about Eric Carle and his books, please visit eric-carle.com
To learn about The Eric Carle Museum of Picture Book Art, please visit carlemuseum.org

ISBN 9781524788674   10 9 8 7 6 5 4 3 2 1

ERIC CARLE'S
BOOK OF MANY
THINGS

world of
ERIC
CARLE™

An Imprint of Penguin Random House

THINGS IN THIS BOOK

THINGS YOU SEE

In the garden · In the sea
On the farm · At home · Weather · In the wild
Things that go · Creepy-crawlies

 ## THINGS YOU EAT

Fruit · Everyday food · Party food

THINGS YOU LEARN

Opposites · Numbers
Shapes · Patterns

 ## COLORFUL THINGS

Red · Blue · Yellow · Green
Pink · Orange · Black and white · Multicolored!

THINGS ABOUT YOU

Your body · Moves you can make · What you wear
Things you can do · Feelings · Having fun with friends!

THINGS YOU SEE

IN THE GARDEN

grass

tree

honeybee

flowers

ball

nest

ladybug

lobster

walrus

narwhal

seahorse

jellyfish

seaweed

reeds

coral

IN THE SEA

octopus

ON THE FARM

crows

farmer

chick

cow

turkey

duck

horse

egg

sheep

lamb

plate

dog

chair

picture

clock

table

cat

AT HOME

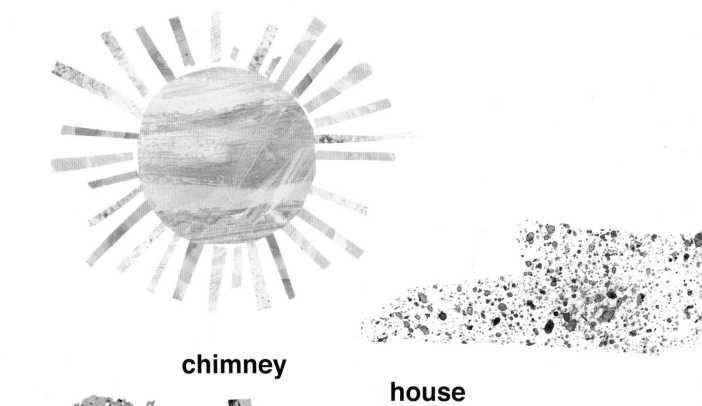

chimney

house

WEATHER

wind

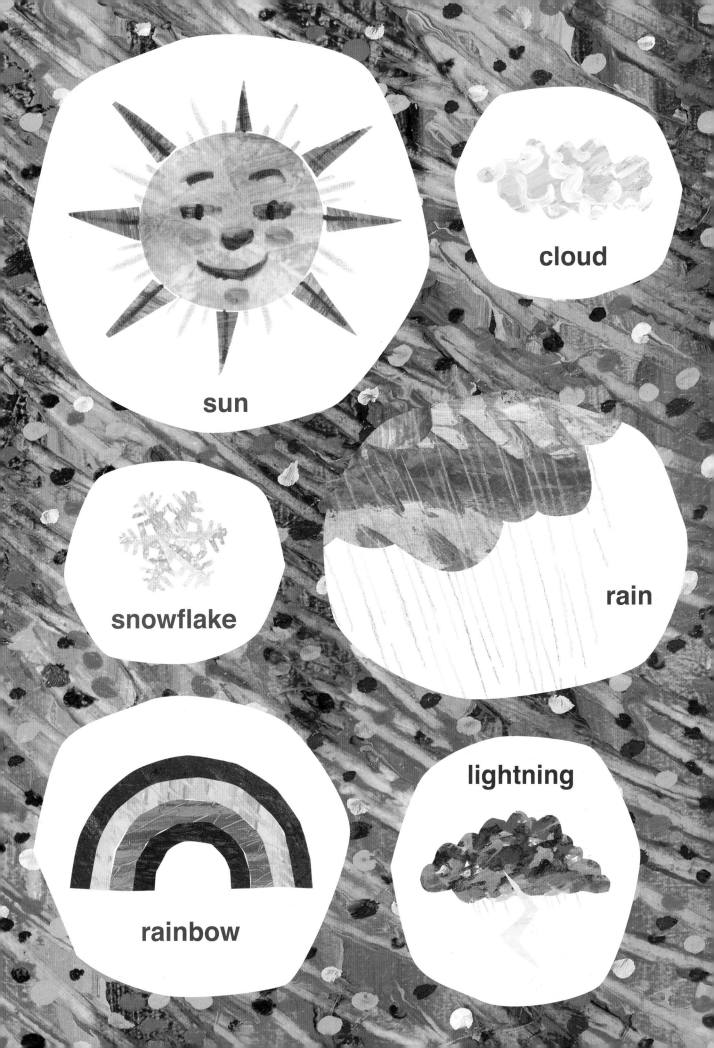

sun

cloud

snowflake

rain

rainbow

lightning

IN THE WILD

snake

rhinoceros

lion

zebra

bear

hippopotamus

monkey

elephant

airplane

truck

car

train

van

THINGS THAT GO

boat

CREEPY-CRAWLIES

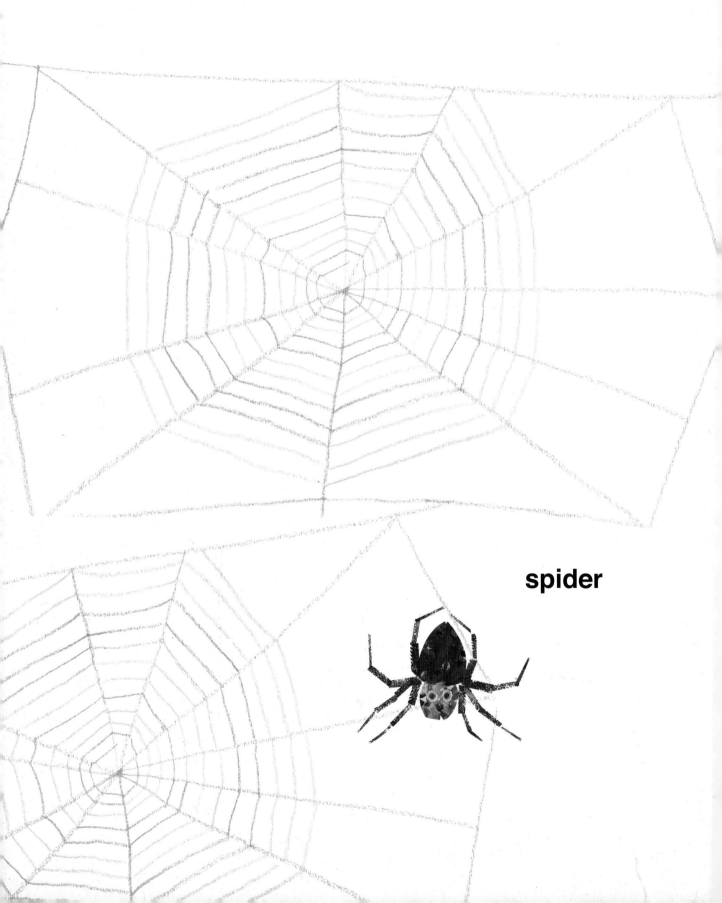

spider

firefly

cricket

snail

caterpillar

fly

beetle

ant

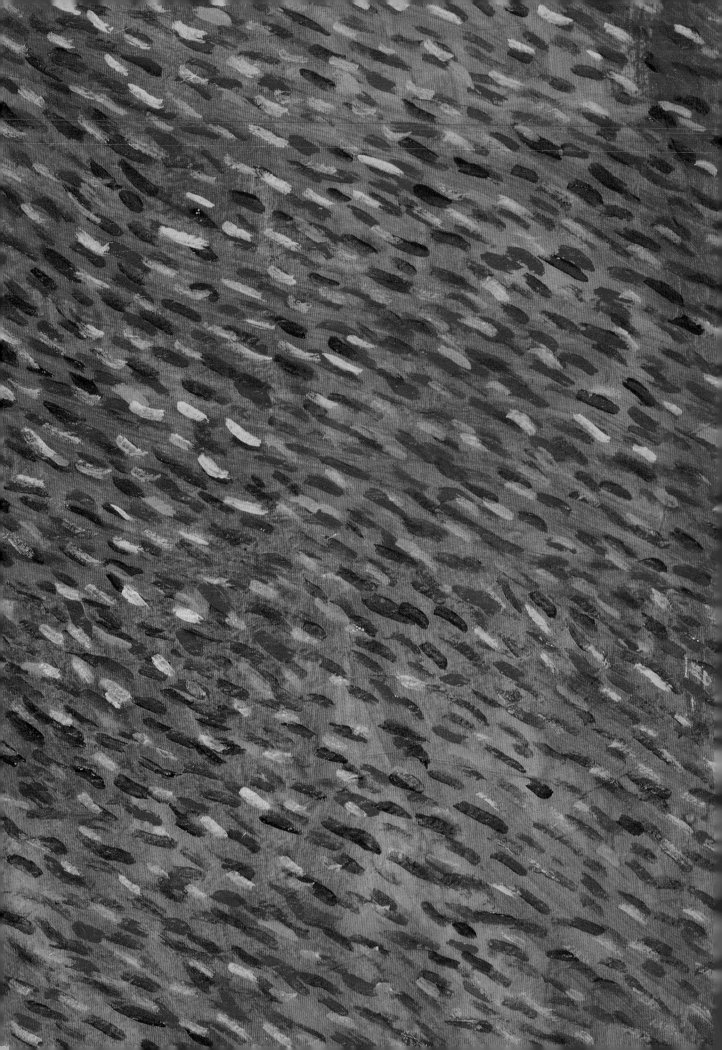

THINGS YOU EAT

FRUIT

watermelon

banana

grapes

lime

pineapple

lemon

kiwi

strawberry

fish

honey

bread

chicken

roast beef

spaghetti

green beans

EVERYDAY FOOD

milk

PARTY FOOD

cake

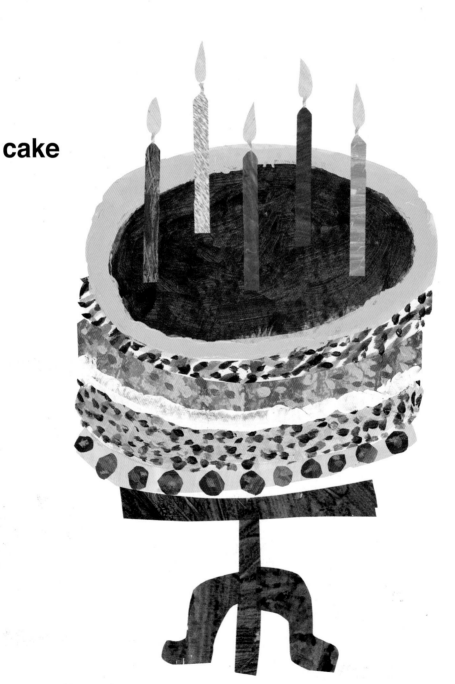

muffin

cheese

pie

ice cream

hot dog

chocolate

THINGS YOU LEARN

OPPOSITES

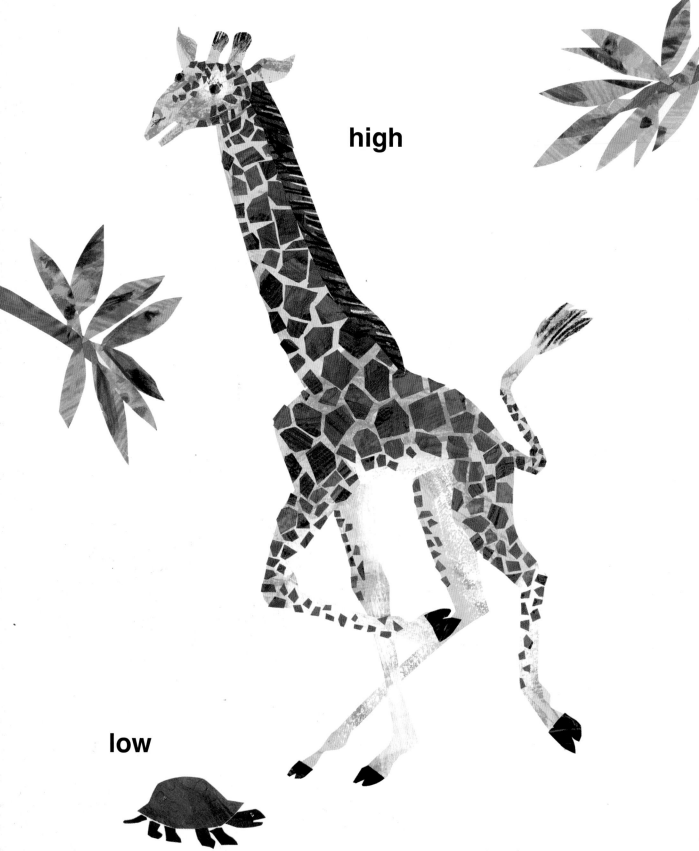

high

low

day

night

many

few

soft

spiky

sweet

sour

big

small

one

two

three

four

five

six

seven

eight

nine

NUMBERS

ten

SHAPES

circles

rectangle

semicircle

heart

square

star

triangle

spirals

spots

waves

splatters

squiggles

plaid

PATTERNS

stripes

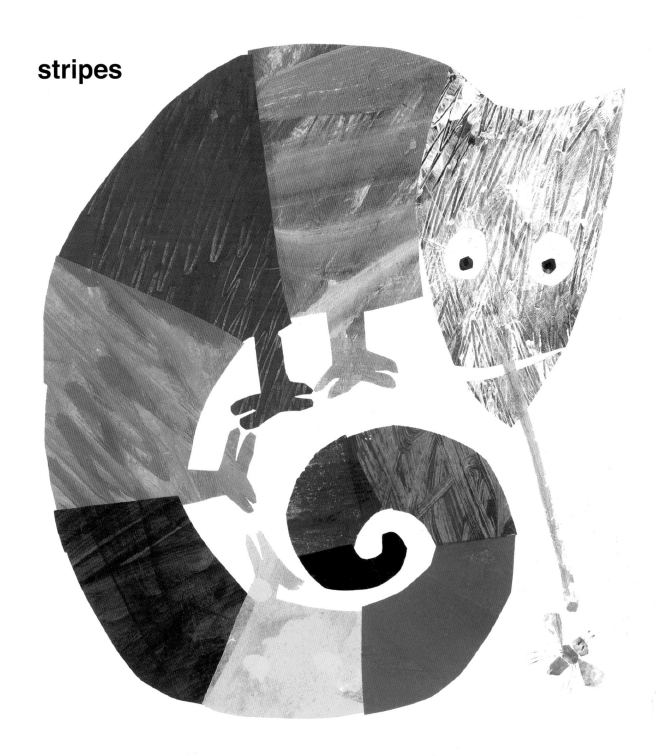

BLUE

dolphin

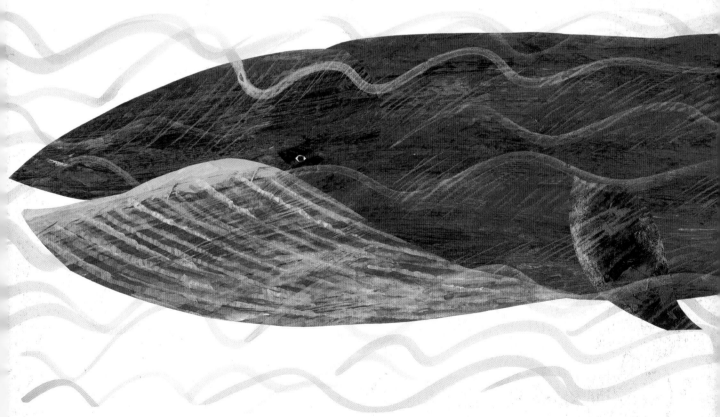

whale

YELLOW

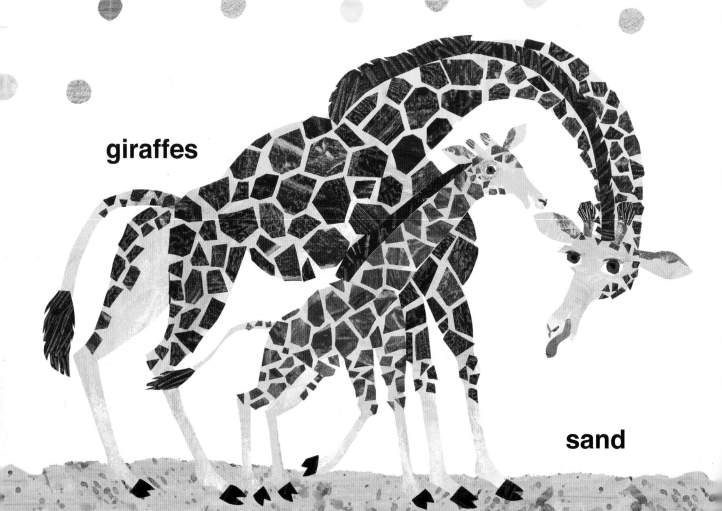

giraffes

sand

leopard

rubber duck

sunflower

bumblebee

lions

leaf

turtle

holly

pear

lizard

pickle

frog

GREEN

crocodile

PINK

blossom

cupcake

pig

flamingo

ORANGE

goldfish

carrots

orange

skunk

panther

panda

goat

swan

penguin

BLACK AND WHITE

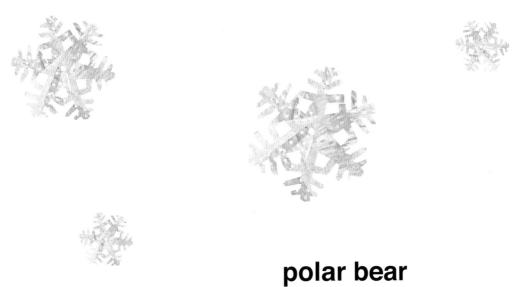

polar bear

MULTICOLORED!

parrot

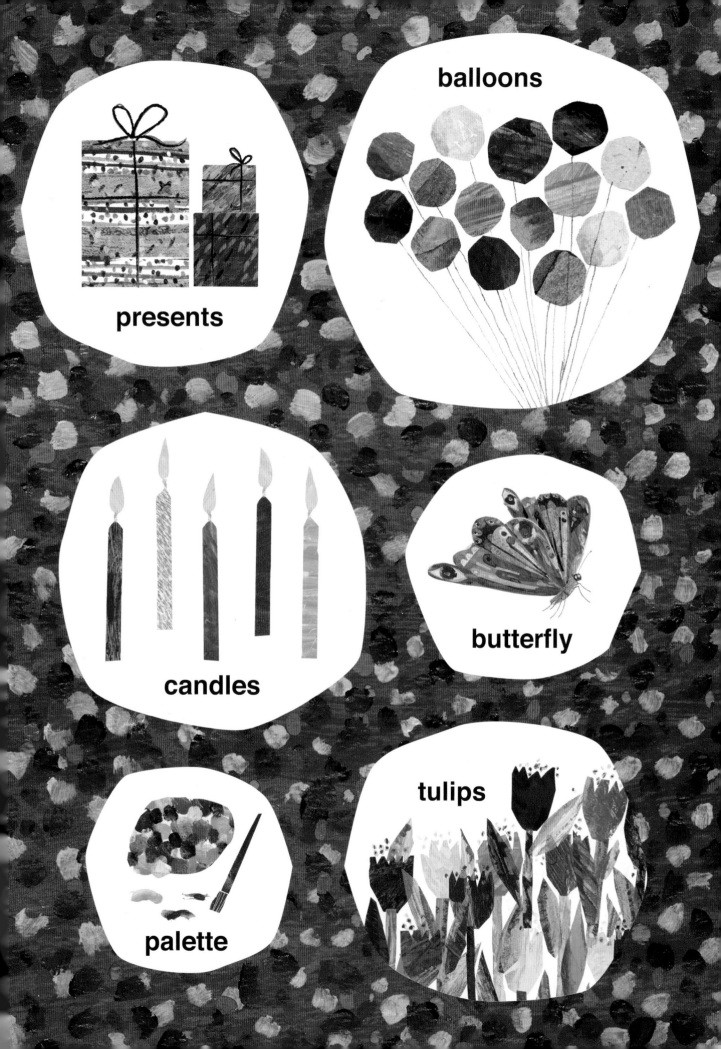

presents

balloons

candles

butterfly

palette

tulips

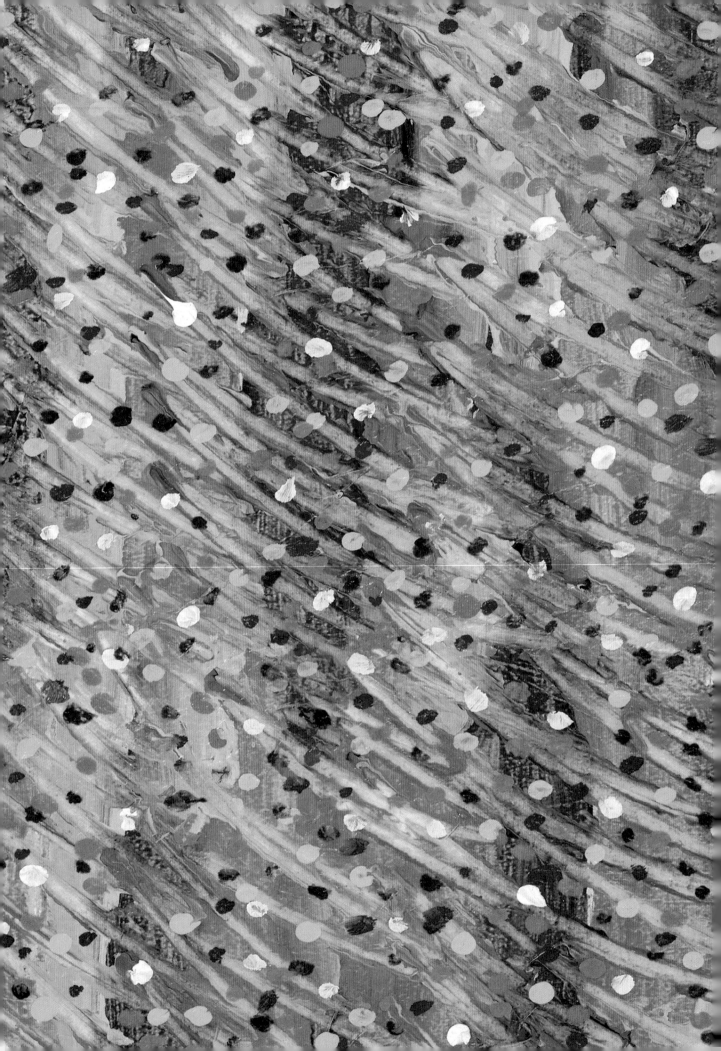

THINGS
ABOUT
YOU

YOUR BODY

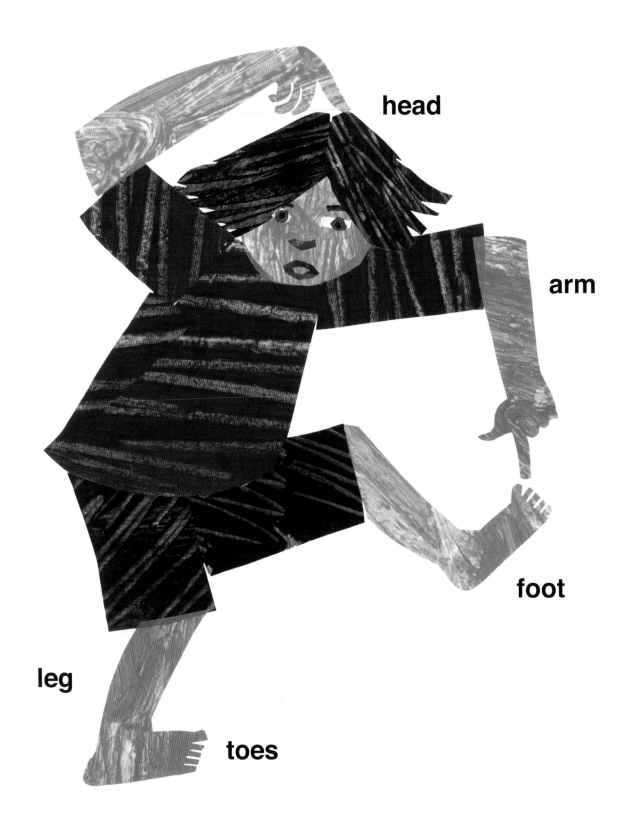

head

arm

foot

leg

toes

shoulder

knee

tummy

hand

dance

run

wiggle

kick

clap

handstand

MOVES YOU CAN MAKE

bend

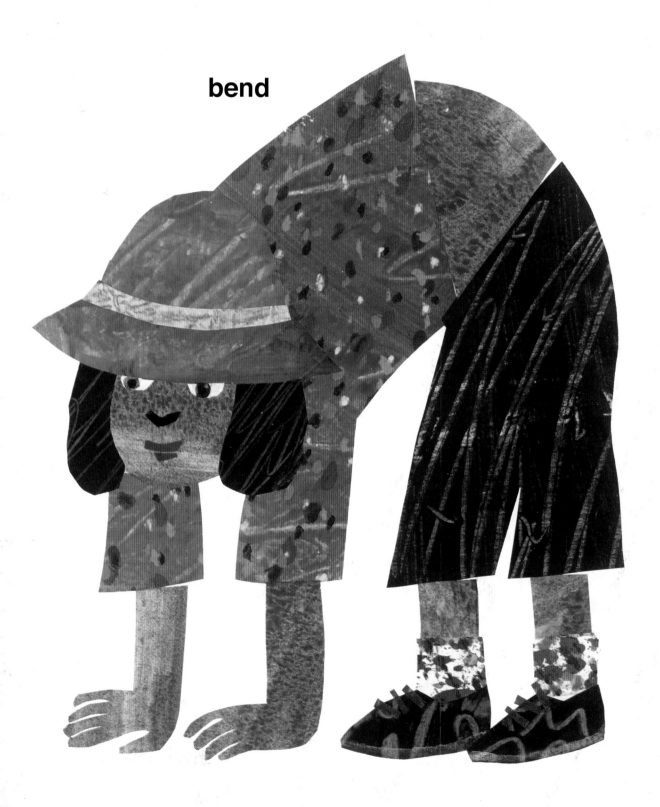

WHAT YOU WEAR

overalls

pants

dress

T-shirt

shoes

hat

vest

glasses

boots

paint

look

sleep

draw

read

touch

THINGS YOU CAN DO

sled

hungry

full

tired

angry

sad

happy

FEELINGS

loved

HAVING FUN
WITH FRIENDS!

share

hug

celebrate

smile

dress up

talk

play

Now, can you name
all these things?